Book Six

of the

by A. J. Atlas
illustrated by Anne Zimanski

Welcome, Readers!

Before you get started, I thought you might like to know a few interesting things about the *Travels with Zozo...*® series. First of all, the stories are set in real places, so the illustrations you'll see try to show the actual landscapes, plants, and animals found in those locations. Second, the cultural and historical elements you'll read about are also as accurate as possible. I hope this knowledge makes the books even more enjoyable for you.

For this story, the setting is the city of Nara, Japan, and the surrounding Kasugayama Primeval Forest. The city was the country's first permanent capital and still contains many temples, shrines, and ruins from its early history dating from 710 A.D.

In a few parts of the story, a teeny bit more creativity and imagination was added. Most of it will be quite obvious, like the board-breaking birds. Other, less obvious, elements that are not 100% accurate include the following:

- Although deer are generally very quiet animals, they are not entirely silent. Occasionally, they snort, grunt, or bleat.

- The illustrations of the ancient buildings were enlarged and condensed for clarity. The rounded green hills in the background were inspired by traditional Japanese art styles.

- There is no grate near the pagoda as shown in the story.

- Tree frogs, deer, and flying squirrels should not be approached, even though Zozo and her family do. It is not safe to go near or try to touch unknown animals.

For the most part, the rest of the information I have presented is accurate and, in my opinion, super interesting! Here are a few more fun facts:

- Approximately 1,300 wild deer roam freely through Nara. They are not domesticated, but visitors can feed special deer crackers to them.

- According to legend, the god Takemikazuchi rode to Nara on a white deer. Since then, the deer inhabiting the forests around Nara were deemed messengers of the gods and carefully protected. People considered seeing them to be a good omen and would bow low to them to show honor to the sacred animal. Over time, the deer learned to bow back, especially if a special deer cracker was involved.

- The world's largest bronze statue of the Buddha Vairocana, known in Japanese as Daibutsu, is in Nara. The statue has the following dimensions:

Statue Height: 49 feet 2 inches (14.98 meters)

Face Height: 17 feet 6 inches (5.33 meters)	Nose Height: 1 foot 8 inches (0.5 meters)
Face Width: 10 feet 5 inches (3.2 meters)	Ears Height: 8 feet 4 inches (2.54 meters)
Weight: 500 tonnes	Eyes Width: 3 feet 4 inches (1.02 meters)

- From when it opened in 752 A.D. until 1998, the building housing Nara's Great Buddha was the largest wooden building in the world. It was built without the use of nails, screws or bolts. Instead, complex wooden joints hold the timbers together.

— AJA

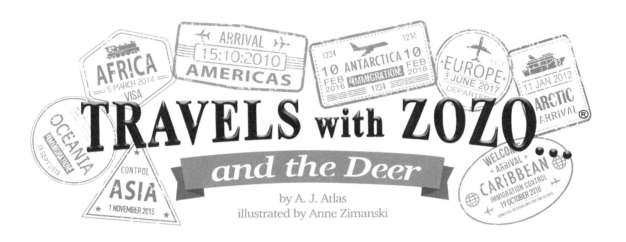

TRAVELS with ZOZO
and the Deer

by A. J. Atlas

illustrated by Anne Zimanski

IMAGINON

BOOKS

Zozo was a hoppity, floppity, huggable, snuggable pet bunny who loved to sleep. She lived with a fun, on-the-run family of four who loved to travel.

Together, they crisscrossed the world sharing
adventures and making new friends.

Zozo and her family were in Japan on their way to the ancient capital city of Nara to learn about its history and culture.

The city was nestled in a wide valley surrounded by
forested hills. As the family looked down from a
hillside hiking trail at the many beautiful places
below, Dad asked, "Where would you like to go first?"

"How about we go see a gigantic statue?" Mom asked. "In the old part of the city, there is one of the biggest bronze Buddha statues in the world!"

Mom reached out and placed her hand over the top of Jazz's head. "In fact, each of the statue's eyes is about as tall as your sister!"

"I'd like to see that!" Jazz and Zozo's brother, Benji, said.

"Me too!" added Jazz.

"Me three!" joked Dad, leading the way toward the city.

Zozo hopped along, passing several tree frogs as they left the forest. One spoke to her with some advice, "When you get to the city, be sure to meet the world-famous wild deer."

Zozo listened as the frog explained, "For centuries, the townspeople protected these deer from harm, believing they were messengers of the gods. Though the deer do not speak, they communicate in many other ways."

Zozo nodded kindly to the tree frog and hopped faster, excited for all that lay ahead.

"Look at that!" Benji said, seeing the city deer for the first time. "The deer and people are *bowing* to each other!" Benji pointed toward several deer in front of a five-storied pagoda.

Amazing! Zozo thought, watching the friendly
exchange of greetings. *I bet I can do that.*

Zozo scooted over to a nearby deer, sat back on her hind legs, and held her front paws by her sides. Then she bent her chest forward while bobbing her head down. She bent so low that she felt the necklace she always wore bob forward with her.

Finishing the bow by straightening back up, Zozo felt the tiny charm on her necklace slide gently back in place as her eyes glanced at the deer. He looked young and small and had many white spots in the soft fur on his back.

The baby deer stood and faced Zozo. Slowly, smoothly, and without making a sound, the deer bowed his head low and raised it back up again. For a brief moment after bowing, their eyes met, and big smiles spread across both their faces.

We did it! Zozo told herself. Excited, she bounced over to another deer. She bowed, the deer bowed, and Zozo bounced on with a happiness in her heart. Bowing and bouncing, bouncing and bowing, she continued to greet deer after deer along the path toward the building with the giant statue.

But in her excitement, she didn't notice when her beloved necklace slipped off and fell through a grate in the ground near the pagoda.

GULP! the baby deer swallowed hard, looking at the lost necklace and then watching Zozo hop further and further away from it. His hooves were too big to reach through the grate to grab it. He wondered how he could help.

Then, he had a idea of how to tell Zozo where her necklace was. He got several other deer together, and they sprang to action. They hurried toward the building with the Buddha statue and caught up to Zozo after she and her family had finished touring it.

One deer made a makeshift necklace from string and a cracker.
The others stacked themselves into a tower to look like the pagoda
Zozo had left. The helpful deer balanced as best they could, but the
tower wobbled side-to-side and back-and-forth. Hoping Zozo would
understand the clue, the baby deer tapped Zozo on the shoulder.

"Oh, hello again," Zozo said, recognizing the baby deer. The baby deer quickly swept his hoof in the direction of the five-tiered tower, guiding Zozo's eyes toward the group's creative message.

But, by the time Zozo turned, the tower had fallen with a thud. The awkwardly squished deer could only manage a weak smile, and the baby deer shrugged his shoulders with disappointment.

Zozo did not realize that the deer were trying to help her. She gave them a friendly bow and hopped away toward her family. She hopped and hopped until she left the deer, the ancient buildings, and unknowingly, her necklace far behind.

Finally, Zozo and her family came to their last sight to see, a red shrine. Zozo felt like she could hop no more and tumbled sleepily into a group of deer resting near the entrance. "Aww, little Zozo, it has been a long, tiring day," Jazz said. "Sleep now, and we will pick you up after we finish visiting this shrine."

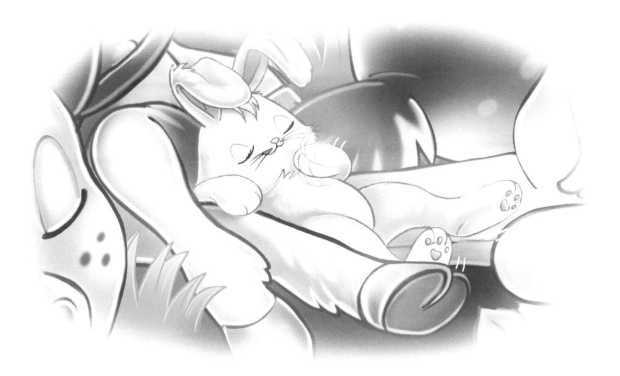

Zozo closed her eyes and relaxed her muscles with a small stretch of her back legs and a little scratch beneath her chin. Suddenly, she was aware that the necklace that her human family had given her long ago was missing.

To Zozo, her necklace was a little sense of belonging. With it gone, sadness replaced tiredness. She bolted upright and cried out, "OH NO! Where's my necklace?"

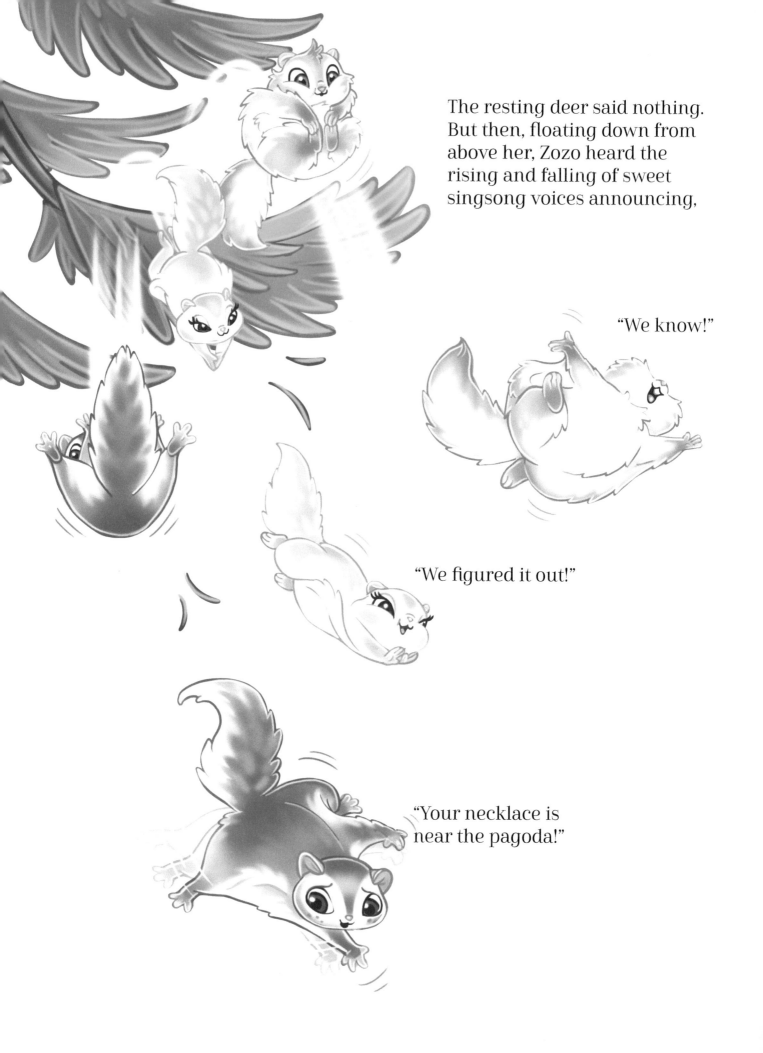

The resting deer said nothing. But then, floating down from above her, Zozo heard the rising and falling of sweet singsong voices announcing,

"We know!"

"We figured it out!"

"Your necklace is near the pagoda!"

Surprised, Zozo watched as three gray-and-white flying squirrels flew down from the tree branches and landed beside her.

"Are you sure?" Zozo asked, confused how these little creatures could know her necklace was far away.

The smallest squirrel came closer, put a friendly arm around Zozo, and confessed, "Honestly, *we* are not exactly sure...but *they* are!" The squirrel pointed her tiny paw toward a group of animals posing in the light of the setting sun.

Zozo turned and saw that the deer from the pagoda had followed her! Once again, they had stacked themselves one on top of another, in the shape of the five-storied pagoda. A cracker necklace dangled in front, and her friend the baby deer smiled at her. Zozo let out a sigh of relief as she understood the message.

Zozo and the three squirrels climbed onto the back of the baby deer as the squirrels introduced themselves. Mimi was the tallest squirrel, Moko was the fluffiest squirrel, and Chibi was the smallest squirrel.

Zozo enjoyed the ride back to the pagoda. She heard stories of the squirrels' lives in Japan and watched when the playful squirrels had fun trying to recreate some of the structures they passed.

Soon, they stood above the grate. Zozo saw her necklace. "We found it!" Mimi proclaimed. Then she easily reached her tiny arm through the slit and grabbed the necklace.

At last holding her beloved necklace in her paws, Zozo thanked the squirrels and the baby deer for their help.

The return trip to the red shrine was filled with laughter
and more fun stories about the squirrels' lives in Japan.

Zozo and her friends arrived back at the red shrine a few minutes before Zozo's family exited. Exhausted but happy, they snuggled back into the group of resting deer.

Looking directly into the eyes of the baby deer, Zozo said gratefully, "Your kind and generous actions spoke louder than any words. Thank you for being my friend."

Meet Zozo's new friends in the next adventure, Travels with Zozo...in the Grand Market!

Travels with Zozo...and the Deer   by A.J. Atlas   illustrated by Anne Zimanski

Published by ImaginOn Books,
an imprint of ImaginOn LLC
www.imaginonbooks.com

Copyright © 2023
by A.J. Atlas

1st Edition
2 4 6 8 10 9 7 5 3 1

Printed
in U.S.A.

978-1-954405-06-6 (Hardcover)   978-1-954405-35-6 (Ebook)

To purchase books or obtain more information about the author, illustrator, or upcoming books, visit www.travelswithzozo.com

Printed in the USA
CPSIA information can be obtained
at www.ICGtesting.com
JSHW041147130224
56968JS00013BA/20